E
ST
Stevenson, Jocelyn

When Grover moved to
Sesame Street

DATE		
AG 12 '87	FE 20 '90	OCT 07 '96
SE 14 87	MR 13 '90	JUL 23 '92
OC 1 '87	JY 23 '90	NOV 13 '97
DE 5 '87	AG 27 '90	JUL 09 '98
AP 6 '88	SE 25 '93	SEP 10 '98
JY 28 '88	NOV 28 '93	DE 21 '99
AG 10 '88	DEC 14 '95	FE 12 '00
NO 3 '88	AB 22 '95	FE 21 '01
AG 4 '89	MAR 01 '96	AG 08 '01
AG 22 '88	MAR 14 '96	AP 07 '03
SE 26 '89	MAY 07 '96	MA 30 '06

© THE BAKER & TAYLOR CO.

When Grover Moved to Sesame Street

CTW

SESAME STREET®

A GROWING-UP BOOK™

When Grover Moved to Sesame Street

By Jocelyn Stevenson • Illustrated by Tom Cooke

Featuring Jim Henson's Sesame Street Muppets

A SESAME STREET / GOLDEN PRESS BOOK

Published by Western Publishing Company, Inc. in conjunction with Children's Television Workshop.

Grover Monster did not always live on Sesame Street.
A long time ago he lived in a different neighborhood,
and his best friend Minnie lived next door.

One day when Grover and Minnie were playing in Grover's room, Grover's mommy walked in.

"Grover," she said, "I have good news. I have a new job."

"Oh, Mommy, that is terrific!" said Grover.

"Yes," she said, "but it means that we must move to a new place—a place called Sesame Street."

"Moving is great!" said Minnie. "You put all your stuff into a big truck, and then you drive to a new house."

"You will have a new room, and you will make new friends!" said Mommy.

"Oh, my goodness!" said Grover. Grover thought moving sounded like a lot of fun.

The next day Grover and his mommy began packing all their things into boxes. Minnie helped.

They packed Grover's cowboy hat and his stick horse.
They packed his ball and his toy robot. Finally, Grover
packed the special clay elephant that Minnie had made
for his birthday.

"Oh, I am so excited!" said Grover as his mommy kissed him good night.

"We are going to move!" he whispered to Teddy Monster. Then Grover looked around his room. It looked empty and strange. "This room does not look like our room any more."

Suddenly Grover felt sad. "Maybe moving is not so much fun after all," sighed Grover as he fell asleep.

The next day Grover ran into the kitchen, where his mommy was packing boxes. "Mommy!" he wailed. "Guess what! Minnie says that she is not coming with us!"

Grover's mommy gave him a big hug. "Of course not, dear," she said. "Minnie will stay here with her family. After we are settled in our new home, Minnie may come to visit us."

On moving day, the biggest truck Grover had ever seen pulled up in front of the house. Grover was so excited he forgot all about being sad.

"Look, Grover," said his mommy. "This is the moving van that will take our things to Sesame Street."

"Please be careful with my elephant," said Grover to the movers. "My friend Minnie made it!"

When the van was loaded and the house was empty,
Grover hugged Minnie good-by.

"I am sorry to move away," sniffed Grover, "but you
can come and visit me on Sesame Street very soon."

So Grover waved good-by to his house, to his street,
and to his friend Minnie.

As Grover and his mommy drove the many miles to Sesame Street, he began to worry again.

"It will not be any fun without Minnie," he said.

"You will make many nice new friends on Sesame Street," she told him. "Just wait and see!"

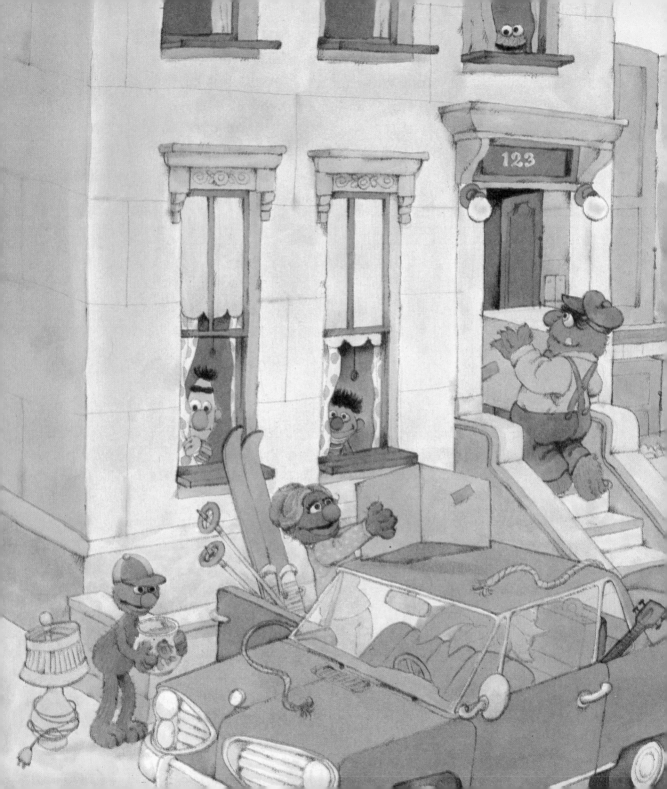

Finally, Grover and his mommy arrived on Sesame Street. The movers took all the boxes out of the van and carried them into the new house. Grover and his mommy brought in the things from the car.

"Let's go to your new room first and unpack all your toys!" said Grover's mommy.

"Oh, goody!" said Grover.

Grover's new room wasn't like his old room at all. It smelled funny. It sounded empty.

"I have changed my mind!" cried Grover. "I do not want to move!"

But his mommy was busy opening boxes. "Oh, look, Grover. Here are your books...and your boots...and your cowboy hat. And here's your clay elephant. Put him in a special place."

Then Grover helped his mommy unpack his boxes.

"There," said Grover's mommy when everything was put away. "That's more like home!"

Grover looked around his new room, and he felt better. "This is a very nice room," he said. "But I wish I had some friends to come and play."

"You will make friends soon, Grover," his mommy said.

Grover went outside and sat on the steps of his house and looked around. "Hello, everybodee!" he said to the empty street. "Grover Monster is here. Where are my new friends?"

He waited and waited, but nobody came along to meet him. Grover wished that he was back in his old neighborhood. He wished it so hard he hurt inside. Grover began to cry.

"Why are you crying?" asked a giant yellow bird.

"I am crying because I do not have any new friends," sobbed Grover.

"Gee, that's terrible," said the bird. "I don't have any new friends either." And he started to cry, too.

"Wait!" said Grover. "I have an idea. I will be your new friend!"

"You will?" said the bird. "Then I will be your new friend! My name is Big Bird."

"My name is Grover Monster."

"Hey, everybody!" Big Bird called down Sesame Street. "Come and meet my new friend Grover Monster!"

Then Big Bird introduced a little girl with braids, two fellows in striped shirts, and a blue monster with round, googly eyes. "Hi, Grover!" they all said. "I'm Betty Lou." "I'm Ernie." "I'm Bert." "Me Cookie Monster."

"Welcome to Sesame Street!"

"Oh, I, Grover, am so glad to meet you."

Grover's new friends took him down Sesame Street to
Hooper's Store.

They showed Grover the Fix-it Shop.

Then they took him to meet a grouch named Oscar, and to see Big Bird's nest.

And as they walked back to Hooper's Store, Grover invited everyone to come and see his new room.

"I think I am going to like it here on Sesame Street,"
Grover told his new friends.